Past Stories

Seventeen Stories From The Past

By: John L. Brown
Copyright © 2021 By: John L. Brown

Introduction

Past Stories from one's imagination, or real? Can be fiction, or something that has really happened. In the stories of this book, you, the reader will decide whether or not you believe it to be fiction, or the truth.

We all daydream about things that make us happy, things that scare us, and to make things better for us in the future. Our imagination is a wonderful thing that we have that can really be magical in a way that can bring new ideas, or it can enslave one's mind to believe something of the unknown.

If you let your mind wander, it can be a beautiful thing. You can learn from it, you can create with it, but mostly, you can go back in time, or into the future. Just let your mind wander to the unknowns of past stories.

Table of Contents

The Railroad Truss

We were teenagers growing up and having fun. Most of us in the neighborhood were at the age where we were getting our driver's license, and we knew we would be able to go other places instead of staying in the neighborhood all of the time. A few of us got our licenses. I got my license, my little brother Jack got his license and Phil got his and we got jobs to make money to buy cars. It didn't take too long before Me, Jack, and Phil had our own car.

We were a little wild sometimes but we didn't get into too much trouble back then. We're older now and get together every now and then and talk about the fun we had as kids in our old neighborhood. I remember the night myself, Jack, Phil, and a couple of other boys went to the old railroad truss about forty miles away. It was known to be haunted and a half man and half sheep was seen by many people, but no one could prove it.

This railroad truss was 200 feet tall and had not been in use for thirty years, according to some older people that lived around the railroad truss. These older people told us they have seen the half man and half sheep before and never went back there. This was scary to teenagers and believing was easy when you were there at night.

It was around midnight we were driving by the railroad truss and me and another boy had to go to the bathroom, so Jack stopped the car and me and the boy got out. When I shut the door, Jack took off leaving me and the other boy there. When the cars headlights moved away from us, you couldn't see your hand in front of your face. It was so scary and we started running behind the car as it got farther and farther away. The only light we could see now, was the sky, but very dim.

Me and the other boy were standing on the road beside the railroad truss, and Jack's car was nowhere in sight. I was mad as hell at my brother for leaving us and swore I was going to get him back. I said to the boy with me, "Paybacks are hell."

We were looking up at the railroad truss, and we could barely see it. Only the outline of it but me and the boy swore we saw something walking on top of the railroad truss. As we stood still, really too afraid to move, something came running at us all of a sudden and we could not see what it was, so we just ran until we were too tired to run anymore. My brother finally came back for us and we cussed him.

When we were pulling into the gas station down the road from our neighborhood, I saw Jack's wallet on the seat next to him because he could never keep it in his pocket, so I picked it up without him seeing me and got out and walked into the gas station because we all knew Kenny the owner well. I told him I was playing a joke on Jack, so he should play along and he agreed. I told everyone that was in the car to say they didn't have any money and everyone agreed. After Kenny pumped five dollars worth of regular, Kenny said, "That'll be five dollars Jack", and Jack reached for his wallet but couldn't find it. He searched the whole car and finally asked us all if we had five dollars between us and everyone said they were broke. We all started laughing, even Kenny was laughing as I said, "Paybacks are hell Jack."

When myself and Jack got home, I told my dad about what had happened and he said, "It's your imagination. There's no such thing as a half man and half sheep, it was probably a deer or dog." I don't know for sure, because the boy and I took off and didn't look back.

Old Cabin Might Be Haunted

My girl-friend and I moved to the mountains of Kentucky where the hunting is great and the land is beautiful. I was scouting around the woods that surround the house for a place to deer hunt. As I was walking slow looking for tracks, I looked ahead and saw an old cabin. As I approached the cabin, I saw that it may have been built in the late 1800s or earlier. It was in very bad condition but it had a beautiful stone chimney on the outside. I looked in the window, and saw a beautiful fireplace. It was too dangerous to go into the cabin, so you could only look through the windows.

After I got back to the house, I told my girl-friend about the cabin and she wanted to go take a look. It was only 100 yards down the hill to the cabin. We walked all around the cabin and we found a well that had bricks stacked around in a perfect circle. Whoever built this cabin did a great job and I guess that's why it has stood till this day. My girl-friend's son looks for treasure with a metal detector and wanted to come and check it out, so the following weekend him and his wife came to visit.

My girl-friend, son, and his wife went down to the cabin and was down there for a couple of hours. When they came back up, her son had found many things, including a penny that was dated 1945 and an old 44 bullet head, so we thought that was the last year someone lived there or shortly after that. Her son found an old button but was too damaged to figure out the age of it.

I was hunting just 30 yards from the old cabin, and it was around 8 or 9 o'clock in the morning. It was windy and I was uphill from the cabin and every now and then I thought I heard soft music and it was coming from the direction of the cabin. I didn't think much about it at the time, because you could hear music on this mountain from anyone's radio playing. I'm a musician myself and I know the difference when someone is singing and a radio playing, this was not a radio, it was someone singing and old song, and there was humming also. I was hunting a little farther from the cabin on this day when I heard the same music. It sounded like an old song but I could not make any words out but it sounded to me, it was a girl singing and a violin playing, there was a hum every now and then and someone else would join in like singing harmony. It was very low and I could barely hear it but when the wind was blowing my way, I heard it much clearer. The song melody sounded like Amazing Grace, and another time it sounded like The Old Rugged Cross because I have heard the music many times through the months I hunted around the cabin. This may sound strange, but I thought it may be someone that lived in that cabin because I could never find the source of the music. I talked to everyone that lived around us and no one plays music, especially at those times.

Now that the above has been told, I want to tell the other part of what happened next. I was heading down towards the cabin because I was going to hunt close by, and when I got close, I stopped and sat down to be quiet because I thought I heard a deer moving and I didn't want to spook it. As I was sitting there, I looked down at the cabin and It was still dark and I could barely see the cabin, but as I was looking, I saw two figures come out of the cabin, one was small, around 5 plus feet and the other was a little taller. They were people and I heard talking but could not make out the words. I knew there was no one else out here because no one can hunt in this area. I was a little nervous because I didn't understand what or who these people were. I just stood still and watched for a few minutes, then I saw them both go to the well my girl-friend and I found behind the cabin just 10 yards away from the back door of the cabin, so I really found this strange, and was starting to think these figures I'm seeing may be ghosts that lived there at one time. The two figures went back in the cabin and I waited for a few minutes and left. I couldn't hunt today after seeing that and decided to do some investigation into the cabin to find out more history on this cabin.

As I was looking in to the history of this cabin, I found out the last date someone had lived there was early 1950s, so the penny was close that my girl-friend's son found with his metal detector. I talked to a few people down the road and in town that knew a couple living there but none of them died in the cabin, so I thought something may have happened much earlier. I was never able to find any more about the history of the cabin, so I let it go. I don't go around it anymore, but my girl-friend goes down there a lot because she likes old stuff and she has found many things from the cabin. There is also another cabin across the road down in the woods but in much worse condition than this cabin, and the only thing still standing is the stone chimney. I've never seen the other cabin, only my girl-friend has seen it.

I believe from what I heard and saw, it was ghosts that were singing, and ghosts that came out of that cabin and went back in to that cabin. Believe it or not.

Fire Cracker In His Pocket

My brother was always playing jokes on all of the guys in our gang. One day he put a black, electric cord down my shirt and told me it was a snake, so I panicked and jumped around trying to get that shirt off and away from my body while my brother and friends were laughing their asses off. I didn't find it funny at all.

I finally got my shirt off with rips all over it and I was mad as hell at my brother and our friends. I told my brother, "You can give someone a heart attack doing something like that," but he just laughed.

I was trying to come up with something that would get him back for what he did to me, so I came up with a fire cracker in his shirt pocket, but was afraid it would hurt him so I decided to just use a fire cracker wick, but he didn't know it was just a wick and not the fire cracker.

The whole gang was out in our front yard and I was standing next to my brother. I waited for the right time to light the wick and drop it in his top shirt pocket. My brother only wore short sleeve button up shirts and they all had a pocket. My chance was now, so I lit the wick and stuck in my brother pocket and he went wild jumping around saying, "is it real?" and I was laughing saying, "yes, it's a real fire cracker." We were all laughing because the wick went out and my brother had the scare of his life, so paybacks are hell, aren't they?

Possum In Your Face

When I was younger, I would do some crazy things that I would never do today. We were a bunch of boys that were wild and everything was fun to us. Every now and then a possum would show up around us and we would kill them because my dad told me they were nasty and shouldn't be in the city, so we killed them when they would come around.

There was a field across from our house where we played football and hung out. My two brothers were there and five of our friends when this possum came from across the street and we all took off after it and one of my friends took off his belt and started swinging it at the possum and slept and fell down right in front of the possum and the possum showed his teeth just inches away from our friend's face, so you should always be careful because you never know when you're going to be on even playing grounds like our friend while staring in the face of that possum's teeth.

My brother grabbed a 4x4 about 4 feet long and he could barely pick it up, but he did and was hitting that possum and it would never die we thought because every time he hit it with that 4x4, it still was kicking. My big brother was tired from swinging that 4x4 at this possum and he said, "This will kill you," and he used all of his might and hit that possum and it finally died. I would never kill a possum or any other small animal. We were young and I thank God we grew up with hearts.

BB Gun And Ground Hog

I had bought my son a bb gun and we were at our favorite farm pond fishing and he took his bb gun and went walking. I was fishing for a while and started wondering where he was, so I searched for him and when I found him, he was shooting a ground hog that was up a small tree about ten feet high. As I walked closer, I saw that poor ground hog with its eye bleeding and little blood spots all over it. I was in shock that my son could do this to a little animal that never bothered anyone.

I took the bb gun away from him and we started walking back to the pond and I was so angry at him and I was yelling at him all the way back to the pond and I saw a snake in the grass next to my foot and yelled at him pointing at the snake and said, "This is what you should be shooting instead of a helpless ground hog." Any other time, that snake would have scared me to death, but this day, I was so angry at my son, it didn't scare me.

When we got home from the pond, I told my wife and she got angry also. I put his bb gun up under my bed and he didn't get it back until he was well over 18 because we all forgot about it until he turned 18. He was 12 years old when he shot the ground hog.

I admit when I got my first bb gun, I shot some birds and a snake but now that I'm older, I would never kill anything I'm not going to eat.

Hotrod Haven

Hotrod Haven is a well-known place
where there have been many people that said
they've seen ghosts there while driving
through it. But it's known mainly because of
a couple that were on their way to a dance
on September 3rd 1950, when they crashed at
the bottom of the hill and were killed. Since
that time, reports claim that the girl has been
seen wandering the roadway and aimlessly
strolling the cemetery at the top of the hill. It
was here that she was buried, side by side
with her young lover. The cemetery at the
top of the road is a private burial ground for
several local families, most notably the
"Mitchell" and "Griffen" families. Since
that time many years ago, this road has
claimed the lives of over 25 people. The
road is winding, twisting, and narrow.

As young teenagers, we went there many
nights driving though there to have
something to do. I personally haven't seen
any ghosts, but many other people have
reported seeing ghosts or something that was
not normal. The time we used to drive

through there was in the late seventies, and the middle eighties. I hadn't been there until 2005 when I met my girlfriend who lived at the bottom of Mitchell Hill Road, and Hotrod haven was just up the hill so I traveled it many times.

I was going to a friend's house up the hill when I passed by the graveyard at the top of the hill. It was very dark and foggy this night and it gave me the creeps. I felt the hair stand up on my back while passing by the graveyard and you had to pass through it very slow because there was a curve at the top.

I made it to the top and to my friend's house where we drank a few beers and just hung out. Around 1 o"clock when I left, it was still very foggy, in fact, you could only go 5 or 10 miles an hour. As I was approaching the graveyard on my left, I saw something floating in air 4 or 5 feet above ground and when I got closer, it got thinner until it disappeared. I can't say it was a ghost, but it was shaped like a woman, and transparent. Before I started dating my girl-friend, she dated a guy up the hill and she

walked that hill at night many times; I could
never walk the hill especially by the
graveyard.

I have a thing for old graveyards and I
really enjoy walking through them during
the day. I like to read the dates and then it
makes me sad for them because they're
dead. There is a roll of markers that are from
the same family there and ages start from 1
to 16 and mst of them died before they were
a year old which I found very hard to
believe. I know during that time these
people were living was hard to live, but this
looked to me like something more sinister
had gone on. I thought maybe the mom or
dad had killed them because times were so
hard and they couldn't afford to feed them
all. I don't know.

I believe there is ghost that roams this
world. I also believe in Ufo's, and I believe
in God. I feel when you die, you become a
ghost for a while until you find your way
and some ghosts never find their way and
roam the world of the living. I feel after
some ghosts can't find their way, eventually
God shows them, and this could explain why

some ghost that were seen a long time ago,
are not seen anymore. Believe it or not, it's
up to you.

Was That A Ghost I Saw?

I was on my way home from fishing all night and was very sleepy but kept going because I wanted to get home to go to bed. My friend Jeremy was with me and we were driving down this country road, and something caught my eye. I looked towards my left in a field where I saw a mound or a small hill and something was floating up from the mound. It was very early morning and during the summer months, grass would have steam coming from it, but this was not steam.

I immediately pulled over and told Jeremy and he said, "let's go check it out." When I first saw it, it looked like a person around 4 or 5 feet high and it was swirling round and round. I could see it was a small person. I could also see through it so it was transparent and so I thought it could be a ghost. I really needed to check this out.

From the road to where the mound was, it was around 60 or so yards in the middle of this field. There was a house 200 yards from the mound and I was afraid someone would call the police on us but went anyway to check it out.

As we climbed the fence, the thing was still hovering over the mound, but a little smaller now, so we kept getting closer. When we got around 20 yards from it, we could see a small person, maybe a girl but not sure. As we got within yards, it completely disappeared in thin air. We checked all around the mound and saw nothing, or anywhere something could come out of the mound. As we started back to the truck, a person yelled out to us and said, "wait a minute, I would like to talk to you," so we waited while the guy walked up to us.

As the guy was walking closer to us, he said you're not the only one that has stopped here, because many, have seen the young ghost and I would always come out to let them know what it is floating over the mound. I said, "what is it?" He started telling me the story. He said, "A little girl, 16 years old, was found buried in this small mound 20 years ago. She had been raped and beaten to death and buried here. There used to be trees all around the mound, but were removed for clearing this field. When the trees were removed, the ghost started appearing daily usually early mornings like today."

I live in the house up there and I have seen her early mornings and late evenings for many years now. Some say, her death was so tragic that she has never found her way and only comes out to search for closure. The guy said, "I feel she doesn't know she is dead. It's very sad." This was the first time I heard about this and found out later that the whole town knew about the little girl ghost.

On the rest of the way home, I couldn't get this little ghost off of my mind and felt very sorry for her. Jeremy said, "she will eventually find her way I hope," and I said, "I hope so too." We don't know what goes on after death and I want to believe that God will help this little ghost find her way, or give her some closure which we believe she is searching for.

Empty Grave

My brother was a grave digger and done it mostly on weekends for the extra money. Sometimes, the grave yard would have him dig the grave a day early when the weather didn't call for rain. My brother told us many times while digging a grave, he felt something near him and there would always be a cold feeling around him. This feeling would only happen every four graves or so but still the same feeling.

My brother was called to dig a grave Friday afternoon so he went and while he was digging the grave with a backhoe, he felt a cold sensation come over him and he felt something near him also. He said he knew something was close and he even said he heard weird sounds of high pitch music from another world, but very soft.

This graveyard was on a road that we would drive through at night because everyone thought it was haunted and everyone that lives around this graveyard tells many stories of seeing ghosts at night.

We were young teenagers always looking for something to do, so five of us got into the car and headed to the graveyard just for something to do this Friday night and knowing my brother had dug a grave early this day was even better because I was telling all of the other guys about the haunted graveyard with an empty grave in it because I knew my brother had dug it that day. The other guys didn't know my brother had dug a grave, so I was going to scare them when we get there. The other guys didn't believe there was an empty grave there.

Not only is the graveyard a very dark and scary place at night, but the road to get there is also just as dark and scary and the road also has many stories of ghosts seen on the road going to the graveyard.

As we were driving the road to the graveyard, no one was talking and kept their eyes on the road because everyone of us wanted to see a ghost, but none showed this night on the way to the graveyard.

We pulled into the graveyard and we all got out of the car and slowly walked towards the empty grave, and we had a couple of flashlights with us also, and we were all very nervous and walking slow and a couple felt their hair standing up on their necks, even I felt that way.

As we approached the empty grave, I said, "turn off the flashlights for a minute," but nobody wanted to turn them off because they were to scared at this point. I was thinking to myself, this is going to scare the hell out of my friends when we walk upon the empty grave, but to my surprise, as soon as we came up to the grave, a small dog started barking and we took off like a bat out of hell before we stopped to figure out what had happened. As we were standing, catching our breath, the little dog was still barking and I felt it might have fallen in and can't get out, so I talked everyone into going back to get the little dog out of the empty grave. They agreed.

When we walked upon the empty grave, we saw it was a tiny, little dog, so we had trouble figuring out which one of us was

going down into the empty grave. No one
wanted to do it, so we decided to hang one
of us down holding their legs, and that was a
problem also, because no one wanted to do
that. I finally said I would do it. But I told
them, if you drop me, I will beat the hell out
of you if you don't get me out fast, so
everyone agreed. Before we started, I decide
to check around the building for some kind
of a ladder, and we found an old wooden
ladder that we used to get the little dog out
of the empty grave.

I took this little dog home and it was such
a friendly dog and I kept it until it died many
years later from old age. I used to tell every
that this dog came from and empty grave,
they never believed me, by I told them it's a
true story.

Scary Dream So Real

I'm really scared of snakes, not when I see them, but the kind you don't see. I was always afraid of walking in the woods or in tall grass because I knew snakes were in there during summer. If I see a snake, I'm not so afraid of it because I can see it.

I went to bed very tired on this night, and just a day or so before, I had seen some snakes that scared me. I didn't know it at the time that I would have a dream of snakes soon.

I fell off to sleep as I normally did and found myself frozen to the bed paralyzed in fright because for some reason, I could not move and there were snakes coming out of a hole in my chest. I was so terrified with fright, and had to just lay there and watch these snakes going in and out of my chest.

I read some articles on dreams and found out that in some stages of sleeping, your body is paralyzed, so I guess I was in that stage but what about me being awake?

I was completely awake during this dream while I was in this state. I tried to move but there was nothing I could do. I was hoping I would wake up, but I was already awake in my mind, so I thought it was real.

I felt snakes moving all around my body, around my hands and still I could not do anything about it. I had to just lay there and let the snakes move all over me.

I have had similar dreams where I could not move, but none like this one because I really thought it was real. While in this state, I thought I was going to die from snake bites or my heart was going to explode with fear. I thought I was going to die of fright.

I didn't know if this was real or I was just dreaming because it felt so real. I know when I have had other dreams, and I would wake up, I could remember them the next day, but if I woke up during a dream and went back to sleep, I could never remember it.

Everything went dark and when I was waking up, I felt and my arms and legs were able to move now, but my heart was beating so fast and there was pressure in my head. I was shaking so bad, that I could not take a drink of water that I had by my bed because it was spilling out of the glass.

I got out of bed and remembered everything and was still terrified to even think about going back to sleep. I just sat in a chair and stayed up until daylight. I was still nervous into the next day because this dream was so real to me and still is to this day. I worry now when I see something that scares me because I'm afraid of having a dream like this one about it.

I have had dreams where I could not move before, like the one where I woke up and someone was holding my mouth and my head down, but I woke up quick and it was over, but this dream was the worst dream I have ever had and I'm so scared now of having another one like this one.

I don't call this dream a nightmare because it was so real. I know people have similar dreams. I searched for some answers and found there are three types of dreaming.

Type # 1. Dreaming is Passive Imagination:

Type # 2. Dream Illusions:

Type # 3. Dream-Hallucinations:

I don't know if my dream is in any of these types of dreaming, because it was so real. I was awake during this dream and no one can explain it to me, not even my doctor.

The Burnt Souls Of The Woods

Have you ever seen something that you just can't explain without someone thinking you're nuts? I mean something that even you can't believe or grasp in your mind, something so unbelievable and no way to really explain without losing your logical mind.

I was deer hunting with a couple of buddies of mine, Rick and Joe, and we were hunting a vast area of woods where it was very dark at night, and scary. I remember hearing coyotes just before going to hunt.

I was walking to my hunting area that was a long way from the other hunters and I could feel my hair standing up on my neck as I was walking through the dark woods. I remember I could barely see with just the moonlight. As I got within 100 yards of where I was going to hunt, I saw dark shadows moving through the woods. These shadows were in the shape of people. There were two girls around 5 feet tall and more than a few males because they were all bunched up together and it was hard to tell just how many there were. I heard soft giggles and whispers. These shadows were not aware I was there, so I was not that scared at this point.

I stood still, watching these shadows and thought I had nothing to worry about. I could not see any faces, just shadow-shaped silhouettes. I had no reason to believe they were anything but humans. It was dark and I just couldn't see their face features. I moved a little closer and I still couldn't make out any faces, but I did wonder why these people didn't have coats on because it was very cold to be out there with a dress on only. I started getting a little concerned to what was really going on there, and why these people are out in these woods that is so far away from any town or city.

I reached in my pack and got my radio and called Rick and told him what I was seeing, and he said, "Just stay there and I will get Joe and we will come to you. I said, "Ok, but hurry." Rick knew where I was going to hunt because we always let each other know where we were going to hunt for safety reasons.

I knew it would take Rick and Joe around ten minutes or so to get to where I'm at, so I just sat down and leaned against a tree and just watched the shadows. It looked to me like they were all very close and it was like a meeting or a get together or something. It was like they haven't seen each other in a while. I wanted Rick and Joe to see this because if I was the only one that had seen this, no one would believe me.

I heard Rick and Joe coming because of the dried leaves and small tree branches that would crack as they stepped on them. The shadows were still there and it seemed to me that nothing bothered them. Rick got down on his knees and Joe stayed behind the tree where I was sitting. Rick said, "I thought you might be pulling a prank, but I see, you're not." We couldn't believe our eyes.

We just sat there watching to see what would happen next.

It was starting to get daylight now, so we could see much better and the shadows were becoming more clearer and we could see facial features but still dark. Their clothes looked to us to be black with lighter streaks, torn in many places. Their faces had black marks up and down like charcoal spots, and it looked like they made these spots themselves, kind of like the Indians used war paint. We could see now that there were two girls and four boys, and they all looked young, maybe in their teens. As it got lighter, the shadows started walking away from us until they just evaporated in thin air, and just disappeared.

We had a hard time taking this in and we all knew this was not normal, and wondered if we should tell anyone, but we thought, there are three of us that had seen this, so others will believe it. We never hunted this morning and went back to the truck and just took a nap. After waking up, we went to the store about ten miles away to get something to eat, and we thought we would hunt the second hunt this evening.

The store had many trucks parked in the parking lot, so I told Rick, "I don't think we should say anything." Rick said, "I saw it, you saw it and so did Joe, why won't they believe us." I agreed and told the story to the store keeper and many other deer hunters standing around listening, and when I said what I had seen, the store keeper said, "hold up a minute" and went to get his dad in the back of the store. He was an older man in his eighties. He came out and said, "what you saw were two girls and four boys that were together at a log cabin just minutes away from where you saw them, that burned down while the girl's daddy went to town in a horse and wagon in 1865 to sell his moonshine and the kids were drinking their daddy's moonshine and having fun, but something went wrong and the cabin started fire while they were all asleep. The daddy came home to find his cabin gone and his daughters with it. The sheriff came to investigate and found there were four boys that had also died in the fire. After the investigation was over, the sheriff found a dead cat by a coal-oil lamp that had been turned over on the floor so he said it looked like while the kids were sleeping, the cat had turned over the coal-oil lamp and started the fire.

To this day the old man said, "you're not the only ones that have seen the girls and boys in the woods, they have appeared in each county around us for many years. Some people would not say anything out of fear of people thinking their nuts, but eventually tell their story."

I know now why they had dark clothes and charcoal faces. The old man said, "we call them the burnt souls of the woods. It's sad, but true."

Man Hovering

I was on my way to visit my friends at a cabin on the lake. I will travel most of the night to get there so I knew I would be up all night, driving. It started raining very hard and rained for over two hours straight, and as I drove over a bridge, I saw the water up to the bottom of the bridge so the water was up.

I was getting sleepy but ignored it and opened a coke to drink for the caffeine to keep me awake. As I was going down this road, I saw on my right, a man hovering over me and dressed in white clothing. I thought it was just my window that was dirty, so I rolled it down and the man was still hovering alongside my car and moving along with me. One minute the man was there, and the next, he was gone.

I pulled over because I had to go to the bathroom and saw the man hovering over me again, so I had a hard time going to the bathroom while the man was hovering over me. I thought to myself, is this a ghost, or an angel looking over me? I was not really afraid of the man, but wondered why he was here.

I was driving way too fast for these winding country roads but didn't think much about it. I remember seeing the man on my left and then on my right again. I was really starting to think, there's something to this man. Maybe he is trying to tell me something. I didn't know.

I went around a sharp curve and almost lost control, but as I was about to go off the road, the man hovering shifted to my left and when I saw him on my left, I turned the wheel in his direction and got my car under control. This made me think, this man is watching over me for some reason so I thought he could be an angel from God. I felt completely safe while this man was hovering over me.

I drove for another twenty miles or so without seeing the man, so I got a little worried because the roads were slick and water was up in spots everywhere. I couldn't help but think this man was here to keep me safe, but why haven't I seen him for a while

I only had forty miles to go and I was hungry, so I pulled over at this small country diner to get a quick sandwich to go. I talked to a couple there while waiting for my order that told me the road and bridge was washed out ahead, so make sure to take a left before entering on to the bridge or you'll drive into the river. I thanked them and went on.

I was eating while driving and wondered about the man which I hadn't seen in a while. I finished eating and lit a cigarette, and dropped my lighter on the floor so I reached down to find it but when I looked up, the man was hovering right in front of me and my hand turned the steering wheel to the left which put me on the road the couple had told me to take instead of taking the bridge because it was washed out. This man hovering over me had saved me twice tonight. I drove very carefully the rest of the way there and never saw the man hover over me again.

I told the story to my friends and they all told me it was an angel from God looking over me. I believe it was an angel.

Night Boat Trip

We were heading to Madison county by boat from Louisville. We took off around eleven o'clock and it was dark and a little foggy which the river most nights was foggy. It was a warm night with a light wind. I saw many lights all around the banks and some on the water from other boats, some fishermen, and some passing by. It was about twenty minutes into our trip when for some reason, there were no lights in any direction, not even on the banks. This was kind of spooky and the other guys thought the same.

We were the only boat on the river we thought and then out of nowhere, a light flashed right at our boat and got bigger and brighter as it approached us. We were getting scared because we thought it was going to hit us. It came within ten feet from us and turned and passed us by. The light went out and we could see the boat which was a ship of some kind that had no lights on, or no crew from what we could see. We could almost touch this ship because it was so close and we were afraid it would sink us, so we moved away from it.

The ship looked like it was very rusty and there were many things missing on the deck that should have been on a working ship. It looked like a ship that had been sitting anchored for a long time. It just didn't look like a real working ship. Mike said, "it looks like the ghost ship everyone was talking about, the Circle Line V." It was all over the internet for a while. It did look like a ghost ship I thought, but why did it have a light shining on us at first? We couldn't explain that. Only after the ship passed us the light went out.

We slowed down and just floated around the ship. There were no lights on and no one was onboard that we could see. We yelled and pointed our spot light at the ship but no response. While our boat was alongside the ship. It was around thirty feet to the deck, so there was no way we could board it without a ladder or rope, which we had no rope or ladder. We decided to get going on our trip and to forget about the ship and as we were moving away from the ship, it just vanished, I mean vanished. One second it was there, and the next second, it was gone. We knew there was something to this ship now.

After we got back home from our trip, we all searched online for anything we could find on the ghost ship of the Ohio river and found it to be the Circle Line V. originally launched in Delaware in 1902. It was amazing to read about something we had seen on the Ohio river that night until it vanished before our eyes. It wasn't one person that saw it that night, there were four other guys with me that night. We couldn't all be seeing things.

Visit A Graveyard At Night

When you're out at night, always be alert
to your surroundings because you never
know when you're going to see a ghost or
something not normal. I believe there are
ghosts among us that we don't see because
we're not paying attention or we just don't
believe there are ghosts. We live in a world
where ghosts are not something we think of
or even believe in so we overlook things that
are not normal.

Think of it this way, you should never say
there isn't any ghost, because there are
thousands of people over the years claiming
to have seen a ghost or something not
normal. Can they all be wrong?

I believe in angels, ghosts, and other
dementions all around us that we normally
don't look for or even believe in.

Go to a graveyard at night around
midnight and sit down and be very quiet for
a while. Keep your eyes open and just look
around. If you sit there long enough, you
will see something. The dead have a way to

communicate just like the living. Some say they are lost souls looking for their way, and some say they're ghost that want to come out at night just to be with other ghosts. Take a flashlight with you and while sitting down, shine it through the graveyard all around the graves, and you will see strange things happen. Believe it or not, it's up to you, the reader of this story.

Ghosts Stories

Growing up I heard many stories of people seeing ghosts. Some were haunted houses where people lived there until they see the ghosts and move away afraid to live there anymore. Some stay in these haunted houses to know more about them. These people aren't afraid of the unknown.

Do a search on the internet and you'll find many ghost stories, some true, and some not so true, meaning that there are a lot of made-up ghost stories. There are also many stories that more than one witnessed it so it's hard not to believe it. It takes two witnesses to convict a criminal, so why can't two witnesses to a ghost sighting be true?

We live in a world where we're not supposed to believe in such nonsense, but some stories are really hard to disregard because more than one person had seen the same ghost many times.

There is a story here in Kentucky where a couple were on their way to a dance in 1950 when the car went off the road, and they were both killed. It's been reported more than once seeing the girl on the side of the road where the accident happened. How can you explain that? True or not true? I personally saw something hovering over a grave while passing a graveyard, in fact, this is the same graveyard the girl and boy are buried in that died in a car wreck in 1950 which she has been seen by multiple people over the years. What I saw was something hovering over the grave marker, and it was around 5 feet. It looked to me, it was a girl with very long hair, and as I passed by it vanished. I can't explain it, but I saw something there that night.

Everyone should have an open mind when it comes to ghosts, angels or other dementions. There could be many dementions all around us and we don't even know it or believe it could be, because we don't want to think about the unknowns of our world. Ghosts and angels are around us everywhere we go. We're never alone. Our loved ones that have passed on are around us, and guide us like angels.

Ghosts are as real as I'm writing this story. As real as you live and talk. Believe in something that is taught us to not believe and you will see more ghosts. Ghost won't hurt us, they just exist. Do right and live right and you will hear from angels that are there to help you.

Finding a place to enter another demention is another story in itself. I believe they exist, but finding one is near to impossible, but I keep searching.

Strange Sounds Under The Porch

We had a deck porch on the back of the house and she wanted it screened in so I re-enforced the post and built walls up around it with eight windows and this was where we would have our coffee every morning. This day was like all of the rest of the times we would have coffee. I heard something but barely, and it seemed to come from under the floor, so we were quiet and we heard it again but much louder now. It stopped for a minute so we thought nothing about it. A few minutes later, the noise started again and then it stopped.

I went to get another cup of coffee and heard it again and this time I knew it was under the porch. It sounded like an eagle at times, then like a baby crying, sometimes it sounded like a high pitch ghost howling.

After we finished our coffee, we decided to check it out. To get under this screened in porch, I would have to take one of the two by sixes from the bottom. I knew I would not fit under it, so my girl-friend went under

to see what it was. This house years ago had
an old cistern under this porch and when she
got over the top of it, she shined a flashlight
into the cistern and there was a baby raccoon
that had fallen in and was holding on to a
pipe sticking out. There was water in there
because of rain and if it would have fallen in
the water, it would have drowned.

We were afraid it would bite her, so I had
to come up with something to get it out
without it bitting her, so I had this old square
wood crate 12x12x12 that I put a handle on
it 3 feet long so she could keep the raccoon
away from her and as soon as she put it
down close to the baby raccoon, it climbed
into the crate and she brought it out from
under the porch and it took off. I'll bet you
were thinking it was going to be a ghost.
Just a baby raccoon that was saved for
another day. We also found out why we had
a few baby cats that went missing, they must
have fallen into the cistern. I cut a 4x8 piece
of 3/4" plywood in half and covered the
cistern and placed three concret blocks on
top so nothing would ever fall in there again.

The Book of Imagination

Victoria Morales disappeared on October 8th

Her social worker, Ms Andrews had made the long drive to Ashdale with a sulky Victoria five days before she disappeared. With barely a word but plenty of paperwork, Ms Andrews left the fourteen year-old with her Aunt Gertrude, who lived in a grand old house in what felt like the middle of nowhere.

Five days later, Vicky was gone and Ms Andrews had to make the drive again, this time with the local sheriff following her.

When the deputy went through the small, neat and very pink room Aunt Gertie had set aside for Vicky, he failed to find anything of interest at all. A small worn backpack with some clothes. A battered old book filled with blank pages. Vicky had had no phone or laptop after the fire which had killed her parents, and there was no clue in the room as to her disappearance.

Poor Aunt Gertie was beside herself with worry and kept re-iterating to the Sheriff, "She wouldn't runaway. I'm sure she's just hiding."

Strangely, Ms Andrews felt more than a small measure of guilt. She had left the girl there afterall, with only a cursory look at the house. Perhaps she had gone wandering in the fields near the house and someone had grabbed her? A weight of worry and fear pressed down on Ms Andrews.

So, perhaps even more than Aunt Gertie, Ms Andrews was delighted when she got a message two days later that Vicky had returned. For the third time she drove out to Ashdale, a mix of relief and anger raging in her heart. Had the girl runaway?

The Sheriff was already there when Ms Andrews arrived and several deputies were standing outside with dogs, all talking quietly. Something was clearly wrong. Ms Andrews hurried inside and spotted Vicky immediately.

She was sitting on a large armchair, and she had a thick blanket wrapped around her. Aunt Gertie was handing her a hot cup of tea. Vicky looked like she had been through something traumatic. Her eyes were wide, her hair was in disarray and her sneakers were covered in mud. Just as Ms Andrews entered the room, Vicky shouted, "It's happening again!"

Everyone turned to stare at her and Aunt Gertie shrieked, snatching away the mug. Startled, Ms Andrews added her own shriek as Vicky disappeared. Right in front of them. It wasn't like in the movies. There was no pop or crack. Just one moment she was there and then she wasn't. The Sheriff shouted at his deputies outside and they all took off with a dog, heading in different directions.

"What on earth is going on?" Ms Andrews demanded, her heart racing. "Where, … what happened?"

Gruffly, the Sheriff snapped, "It keeps happening. Every couple of hours. One second she's here, the next… out in the fields somewhere. She was hysterical when the deputy found her. She kept screaming about talking rocks and fading away."

Ms Andrews stared at him, certain the man was crazy himself. "What?"

"If I hadn't seen it with my own eyes, I wouldn't believe it either. She's disappeared three times since we first found her," the Sheriff growled, running his hand over his crewcut. "I have no idea what's going on!"

From across the room, Aunt Gertie sobbed, "It's the book. It has to be!"

Both the Sheriff and Ms Andrews stared at her, their expressions a picture of shock. "What?" Ms Andrews snapped, her patience short.

Gertie pointed at the thick book Ms Andrews recognised as the one they had found in Vicky's room. "My father swore his uncle disappeared and it was the books fault."

The Sheriff snorted in disbelief but then shook his head. He did have a disappearing girl after all. "What book is it?" Aunty Gertie nudged it with her foot and replied, "That's just it. I don't know. It's blank. No title, no words, no anything."

Sceptical, Ms Andrews snatched up the book and Aunt Gertie cried out, as if she expected something magical and awful to happen. Nothing did, but Ms Andrews was nonetheless cautious as she opened the book. It was indeed blank, and it felt old, and heavy. "Really, this book is magical?" Ms Andrews asked.

Aunt Gertie shrugged, "It has to be. Uncle Victor never came back…." She trailed off as a deputy returned. His face was red and sweaty and he said, "We found her again, Sheriff. She's hysterical and fighting us, screaming that she wants to go back."

All three adults stared at him and then Ms Andrews, who still had the book open, screamed. A large pair of eyes had appeared on the blank page. Eyes that looked alien and dark, etched in black ink. She dropped the book with another scream. She wasn't the only one. Off in the distance, they could all hear Vicky screaming, "Let me go! Let me go back!"

The eyes in the book disappeared and several seconds later the other deputies dragged Vicky inside. Ms Andrews stared at her, stunned. It was definitely Vicky but she was wearing different clothes and looked older. Her hair was short and she was taller too. When Vicky spotted the book, she shouted and with surprising strength tore away from the deputies. Snatching up the book, Vicky glared at all of the adults around her and said, "I'm here, I'm here!"

For a long, long moment nothing happened and then, the book fell to the floor. Vicky was gone. Perhaps because the book was open now when it happened, they all saw a figure move across the page, a figure that looked a lot like Vicky. She ran from left to right and vanished.

Vicky never reappeared even though the Sheriff and his deputies searched. Her case was marked as 'Runaway'.

Aunt Gertie locked the book with no name in a cupboard. She failed to notice the letters which shone in the dark, "The Book of Imagination."

My Imagination

After classes on Friday, Jack met me in the hallway and invited me to go hiking during the weekend.

"That'd be great, where do we meet?" I asked him.

"My house at 10 AM, will you make it?"

"Yes, I will. Thanks"

I was quite sure he had also invited my closest friend Jill, and she was the reason I got invited too. Everyone knew Jack had a crush on Jill, except Jill of course- or at least she pretended to.

We gathered in Jack's apartment the next day, and by 10:30 AM we were all set and ready to go. We got to the woods an hour later. We had trekked all the way chatting and laughing. James always tried to take over the conversation, he loved being in the spotlight. He was Mexican and had a nasal ring to his voice.

We set up camp a some distance from the bank of a slow moving river. Jack managed to get Jill engrossed in a conversation and they were both conversing like they were the only two in the world, completely ignorant of everything else except when James tried to interject. So I was left all by myself, with James for a quite annoying company. He always had something to say and he talked too much. He was Jack's friend, so I guess they both planned the trip together.

I was bored, so I tried to think of a game we all could play. Evading Capture came to mind. I suggested this to the group. "Come on," James said "we are not third graders. How'd you even come up with that?"

"Oh then what do we do now?" I said.

"If you are bored then go home" James replied.

"Now come on James," Jill said "don't be so harsh. Honestly it's getting kind of boring and we need some stimulus, a little running around in the woods wouldn't be so bad"

"So you think we should play the game too?" Jack said.

"Hmm mmm. Let's do this!" She replied standing up.

"Okay, so who's gonna be the predator?" Jack said.

"I'll be the predator," James called out.

"Oh yea, you are more predatory likey," I said.

James ignored me and went ahead, "Every one you have ten seconds to hide! Nine!"

Three of us went scurrying into the woods.

"Eight! Seven! Six!"

I quickly found a rock nearby about two meters from where we stood, and hid behind it.

"Five! Four! Three! Two! One!"

I caught something moving out of the corner of my left eye, on closer observation it was a snake. It was green and thin, the type they said was dangerous. The sight of it sent shivers down my spine. I was transfixed. I was at a loss for what to do. The snake crawled onto my feet. I felt it cold and soft crawling up my leg. I was still frozen, my mind blank. It circled by leg and was slithering up my thighs, it got to my torso and then started heading towards my head. I saw the tip of its nose coming close to my nose.

I couldn't stand it anymore. I screamed, "AAAHHHHH!" and flung the snake away from my face. I didn't wait to see where it landed. I started running back towards the others. But I didn't hear any sound. I wasn't even sure anymore which direction I was running towards.

Now I stopped to look around me. Scarier now, I could feel my eyes welling up with tears, I was lost and I had no idea where my friends were. I didn't have my cell phone on me. I left it on my backpack at the campsite when I ran away to hide. "Never leave your phone behind," my dad had said.

I was worried and my muscles ached from all that running. "How would I get out of these woods? Have my friends even realized I'm missing? Oh God what would happen now?

I calmed down a bit and tried to calculate the direction from which I had run. Okay, I remembered I ran northwards, so I should be heading south now. I faced that direction and started heading back. The incident with the snake left me shaken and I didn't want to repeat the experience.

Just then I heard some footsteps to my left. "Jess is that you?" it was Jill. I had never been so happy to see another human being in my life. "It's me!" I answered. My voice sounded strange in my own ears, so shrill and thin.

"Guys she's here!" She called out to the others.

"What happened to you, we've been searching for you for ages. What happened?"

''You suggested we play the game only to get lost in the woods yourself? Now that's funny," James said with a smirk.

Staring at him in mild disbelief "you have a weird sense of humor," Jack said.

"When we went to hide, I decided to hide behind a rock that was just few meters from where we were. But I stumbled upon a snake and ran away from it. That's how I lost my way." I didn't tell them how the snake crawled to my feet and slithered up to my neck. I didn't want to recount the experience.

"You ran away from a snake? You must be really fast. I bet Usain Bolt couldn't beat you at the Olympics," James said laughing at his lame joke.

"Hope it didn't hurt you?" Jill asked with concern. "I had hidden behind a tree when I heard your scream. Everyone else heard it too and we tried to follow the direction of the sound, but we didn't find you. We then started searching for you. Jack tried to reach you on your phone after we had searched for you about fifteen minutes, but we didn't have any signal reception. I'm so sorry Jill. I'm glad we found you."

"We should get going guys the trip is over. Thank God we found Jess." Jack said.

We started to make our way back. We had trekked for about an hour, before we started getting uncomfortable. It was getting darker and our camp site was still not in sight. James spoke up first. "Are you sure where we are going?" he said to jack who seemed to be leading the group.

Jack didn't want to say it but the look on his face informed us that we were lost!.

Jess! Jess! I heard someone calling my name. It was Jill's voice again. I tuned and found her coming towards me. I was there still standing in the hallway.

"What are you doing here standing alone in the hallway? Were you waiting for me?" without waiting to hear my reply, she continued, "Jack invited me to go hiking with him tomorrow. He told me he invited you too. You agreed to go, right?" she asked as we started going down the hallway.

"Yes I did, I'm sure it will be fun."

ISBN 9798740639345
90000
9 798740 639345